UFO DIARY

ISBN 0-590-44416-6

Copyright © 1989 by Satoshi Kitamura.
All rights reserved. Published by Scholastic Inc.,
730 Broadway, New York, NY 10003,
by arrangement with Farrar, Straus and Giroux, Inc.

12 11 10 9 8 7 6 5 4 3 2 1   1 2 3 4 5 6/9

Printed in the U.S.A.   23

First Scholastic printing, February 1991

UFO DIARY

SATOSHI KITAMURA

SCHOLASTIC INC.
New York   Toronto   London   Auckland   Sydney

On Monday, I took a wrong turn in the Milky Way.

There in front of me was a strange blue planet, bright as a glass ball.

**Between white clouds
I saw shifting, changing patterns and**

I flew on toward that patchwork of scattered islands and seas

until I saw a creature.

It stared at me as I landed.

What an odd-looking thing!
It spoke and I could not understand;
but I smiled. It smiled back.
Then I knew he was going to be my friend.

He showed me around and introduced me to his relations.
We played for hours, until it grew dark

and the sky lit up with a million constellations.
We looked up together and I showed him the way I had come.

There was the friendly light of my own planet.

It was time to go home;
but first he wanted to have a ride.

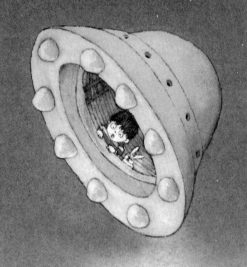

We whirled into the night, spinning around his planet until he was giddy.

I dropped him home and he gave me a present.
It was yellow and grew in the field where we met.

"I'll plant it somewhere," I promised.
He smiled at me and we waved goodbye.

**The planet slipped away beneath me.
It grew smaller and smaller
until at last it had vanished into the darkness of space.**